AF427537

WANTED
For A Good Time
Call TF

Not A Children's Book

The Dark Side Of Nursery Rhymes

Jamie R. Scully

Not A Children's Book - The Dark Side Of Nursery Rhymes

Copyright 2022 - Jamie R. Scully

This book is a work of satirical fiction. While this work satirizes popular nursery rhymes, the events, people, and places in this book are a product of the author's imagination. Any resemblance to actual persons, living or dead, or actual events is purely coincidental. And no, the Tooth Fairy isn't actually a mean, grumpy drunk.

Cover art by Beth Mackenzie Brown and Melissa Wiegand of All The Missing Marbles Art Studio

Edited and published by Ryan D. Hall - Royal Hearts Media

To my loving wife Nicole. I could not have done this without her support. But...she says I'm not funny. You be the judge.

Table Of Contents

Introduction

Hello, I'm The Tooth Fairy and I will be your narrator.

Rumpelstiltskin was supposed to be narrating this thing, but he had more important "business" to attend to. I have never trusted that guy. I heard he steals silverware from restaurants.

Between you and me, I only took this gig because I needed money to pay my bookie. I bet $50,000 that Betty White would see 2022.

We all know and love the classic nursery rhymes that were read to us as kids. But, have you wondered where they came from? I am here to reveal the dark truth.

I have compiled a list of the most popular nursery rhymes. It turns out there are only sixteen. Extensive research, grueling interviews, and loads of sleepless nights went into making this book. I hope you appreciate all my hard work. Creating this masterpiece almost cost me my marriage.

My saving grace is that I am dedicating the book to my wife. I know all of you think that I am a woman. I, The Tooth Fairy, am a man. It is sexist to assume that because I am a fairy I must be a female.

I bet you hear the word nurse and automatically think of a woman. Shame on you. It is 2022, anyone can be anything they want to be. I got enough shit growing up. Do you think I need you judging me? Maybe you're not judging me.

I could be jumping to conclusions. I did a lot of drinking in my 20's and 30's. And some in my 40's. It has clouded my judgment. Fuck, where was I going with this? I lost my train of thought.

Oh yeah, you are helping a good cause. So, 25% of the proceeds from this book go to curing my alcoholism. We can fight this thing together. Enough about me, on to the stories.

Little Miss Muffet

Little Miss Muffet
Sat on a tuffet,
Eating her curds and whey;
Along came a spider
Who sat down beside her
And frightened Miss Muffet away.

Little Miss Muffet was not a child as you may have thought.

She was a Dwarf. Bashful was her second cousin. She owned a fashion design business that specialized in furniture and coats.

It was not just any spider that visited her that day. The spider's name was Big Daddy Long Legs. He was a well-known pimp looking to upgrade his wardrobe. He wanted Miss Muffet's expertise for a new fur coat design.

Little Miss Muffet was terrified of spiders ever since she was a kid. It didn't help that her father had a spider tattoo on his arm. She had been attending Arachnophobes Anonymous for years.

Spider-Man hosted the meetings once a week. I know the meetings are anonymous, but a list got out exposing well-known celebrities.

The list included Optimus Prime, Rainbow Brite, Fozzie Bear, The Green Lantern, Molly Ringwald, Clifford the Big Red Dog, Captain Crunch, Gumby, and Sailor Moon.

As Miss Muffet ran away, she tossed aside her curds and whey. To this day I still do not know what curds and whey are.

The curds and whey landed on Big Daddy Long Legs. It was like swimming in wet cement. He never had a chance. He left behind a wife, 300 children, and 20 hoes. Word got out that a hit was put on Big Daddy.

The hoes tracked down Miss Muffet and forced her into prostitution to support all Big Daddy's children. After a few months, Miss Muffet started doing drugs. She got addicted to cocaine. She lost her design business and started turning tricks to make ends meet.

It wasn't all bad. While on cocaine, she was able to figure out the Rubik's cube and who let the dogs out.

Guys were eager to stick it in her tuffet. I thought a tuffet was her ass too. A tuffet is a stool, who knew? She was found a month later, dead of a drug overdose and two months pregnant. The father is unknown. She leaves behind disappointed parents.

Georgie Porgie

Georgie Porgie, pudding and pie,
Kissed the girls and made them cry,
When the boys came out to play,
Georgie Porgie ran away.

Georgie Porgie was not the cute little pudgy kid you imagined him to be.

He was...that school cafeteria aide. He worked on the lunch line as a food server. He was well known for making delicious pudding and delectable pies. He was more well-known for his inappropriate behavior which made dozens of students feel uncomfortable.

Since I dabbled with journalism in high school, I was able to interview a bunch of former students. Here is what they had to say:

The Tooth Fairy: What was it about Georgie Porgie that made you uncomfortable?

Lisa: He used to blow kisses to all the girls. At first, it was kind of cute because I thought he was mentally challenged. It turns out he is a creepy old man.

Jennifer: He made first-class pudding and pies, and he forced it on you. He would make a big deal out of it if you didn't want to eat his dessert. I tried to bring my lunch as much as I could. I told all my friends to do the same. We did anything to stay far away from that man.

Andrea: As girls, we put up with a lot of shit in high school. Some of these girls could not handle his behavior. They would run off to the bathroom crying. Not me, I'm not a pussy.

Julie: We made several complaints to the principal, but he never got reprimanded or fired. I heard he is the Superintendent's brother-in-law or something.

Monica: Georgie was also one of the monitors at recess. He kept his distance though. The tougher boys would stick up for us and threaten to kick his ass. If the boys got too close to him, he would run away into the woods.

Tyler: I didn't have a problem with him. He loved Science-Fiction. We talked about Star Wars and Time Travel a lot.

All the girls: What the fuck Tyler?!?!

Tyler: Sorry, my bad.

The Tooth Fairy: Yeah Tyler, what the fuck?!? Don't be a dick.

Tyler: I said I was sorry, jeez.

The Tooth Fairy: Is Georgie Porgie his real name?

Samantha: No, his real name is George Porters. I'm not sure who came up with the nickname. It's because he had a big gut. Probably from eating all the leftover pudding and pies. He would get irate if he heard us call him Georgie Porgie. I heard he took that anger home and beat his wife with a wooden spoon.

The Tooth Fairy: Yeah, that is not a fun nickname. Poor Mrs. Porgie. Does anybody know what he is doing now?

Andrea: He still works at the school! My younger cousin goes to that school now. He is still being a creep and hitting on the underage girls.

The Tooth Fairy: Shit, I thought he retired. That is terrible. Someone needs to do something about that creeper. I'll call up my boys He-Man and Robocop to rough him up a bit. They owe me a few favors. I got them to kick their circus peanut addiction. Thank you, girls, for setting the record straight about Georgie Porgie. The world needed to hear the truth.

All the girls: You're welcome!!

Mary Had A Little Lamb

Mary had a little lamb,
Its fleece was white as snow,
And everywhere that Mary went
The lamb was sure to go;
He followed her to school one day—
That was against the rule,
It made the children laugh and play,
To see a lamb at school.

And so the Teacher turned him out,
But still he lingered near,
And waited patiently about,
Till Mary did appear ;
And then he ran to her, and laid
His head upon her arm,
As if he said—' I'm not afraid—
You'll keep me from all harm.'

' What makes the lamb love Mary so ?'
The eager children cry—
' O, Mary loves the lamb, you know,'
The Teacher did reply;—
' And you each gentle animal
In confidence may bind,
And make them follow at your call,
If you are always kind.'

Mary Had a Little Lamb is one of the longest nursery rhymes.

It also has one of the oddest backstories. Mary from 'Mary Had a Little Lamb' was a delusional mental patient. I know that calling a mental patient delusional seems a bit redundant, but she was a bit cuckoo for Cocoa Puffs. Am I allowed to say that, is that copyrighted? Do I need to pay someone a royalty?

In my research, I found some unusual notes from one of the nurses that took care of her. I took a bunch of the notes and compiled them into a little story. My grandpa was right, I am meant to be a writer.

Is it time to finally hang up these wings? Not yet, I think I still have a year left on the lease for this wand. Now that I think about it, I have never even used this wand for anything. It's just for show, like spinning rims.

Mary suffers from delusions and is emotionally unstable. She claims to be a young girl that cares for a flock of sheep. She tells stories of her going to school and getting into trouble with one of the lambs. We have written and recorded a lot of what she has said whilst she is a patient here.

For shits and giggles, we made up this poem about Mary and her lamb. We showed it to Mary, and she loved it. She sings it all the time. A lightbulb went off in my head and I had to publish it. I didn't think it would become a best-seller.

One of the aides thought it would be funny to make a sock puppet lamb and leave it on Mary's bed. Mary lost her mind and broke down crying. She kept saying 'where have you been, where have you been?' Her intimate relationship with that sock creeps us out. She wouldn't go anywhere without it. Once we tried to take it away to wash it. It looked like it had spent some time in the toilet. Mary did not approve and bit one of the aides. We had to restrain her in a straight jacket. She wasn't the same after that incident. She doesn't talk much anymore. She just pets the sock puppet and mumbles to herself. Sometimes we can hear her singing. It is difficult to make out the song. The only words I can ever make out are Little Bo-Peep and something about sheep.

Someone snitched and we all have to speak in front of the board for workplace misconduct. I bet it was Larry. He has had it in for me since I wouldn't put out on that one date we had. I probably deserve what's coming for me anyway. Time to update the ol' resume.

Old Woman Who Lived In A Shoe

There was an old woman who lived in
a shoe.
She had so many children, she didn't
know what to do.
She gave them some broth without
any bread;
Then whipped them all soundly and
put them to bed.

I finally tracked down the 'Old Woman' that this rhyme is about.

I attempted to interview her, but she would not shut up.

I could not take notes fast enough.

I gave her my laptop and let her do her thing.

**

Hey, this is the 'Old Woman' from that famous rhyme, you know the one. I am here to set the record straight.

First off, my name is Rachel. I am 98% sure that my neighbor Doris had something to do with this tall tale.

She never knew my name. And I am not that old! I went gray in my mid-thirties, it's genetic. My mother went gray young and so did her mother. It sucks, but it's a part of my life. I dyed it for years and then decided to embrace it. I never told Doris because she was super nosy, and I never trusted that old bat.

First, I did not live in a shoe! How is that even possible? My house resembled a shoe. My husband is an architect with the creative intuition of an artist. He also shares my affinity for shoes. We wanted a house that was different from everybody else's.

First, we thought about a house in the shape of a pineapple, but that was taken by some guy named Bob.

My husband was away on business all the time. I was always stuck home with the kids. We could not have children the old-fashioned way. His swimmers were slow and couldn't find my eggs with a map.

We adopted ten kids. We are kind of like the original Angelina Jolie and Brad Pitt before they split up. It became an addiction like Angry Birds, we couldn't stop. After we hit ten, we realized we may have gone overboard. Too late, can't take them back now. They frown upon that.

With my husband out of town, it was challenging to find time to grocery shop. This was before the invention of Peapod and Instacart. We had to do it the old-fashioned way and go to the dreaded grocery store. Do you know how difficult it is to go shopping with ten kids by yourself?

I had to get creative and use what was already in the kitchen. I remember one night the cupboards were barren. I found leftover broth from another dinner. I poured it into one big bowl and stuck ten straws in it. Did I mention how much I hate doing dishes? I would rather watch 24 hours straight of the Jersey Shore than do a load of dishes.

At some point during dinner, my firstborn started asking for bread. I told him they ate it all for lunch. As a result, what did he do? He started a chant. They were all banging the table screaming 'we want bread, we want bread!'

Doris must have heard all the commotion and came waltzing over. I reluctantly opened the door. The look on her face, after seeing the kids drinking their dinner, was priceless. To this day, I wish I had clocked her right in that smug face.

Well, she's dead now, I guess I have the last laugh. Was that too harsh? I don't care, fuck that bitch.

To be clear, I have never whipped my children. The occasional spanking, yes. But never with a whip.

I do HAVE a whip. My husband and I use it in the bedroom when we want to play Raiders of the Lost Ark. He is one sexy Indiana Jones.

I don't know how Doris would have known that I had a whip or maybe it's just a coincidence. At least she doesn't know about the boulder. That thing is tough to hide.

I guess the secret's out. My husband is going to kill me. I hope that clears up that nonsense.

**

To all women named Doris, I apologize on Rachel's behalf. I knew nobody could live in a shoe. It all makes sense now.

The Muffin
Man

Do you know the muffin man,
The muffin man, the muffin man,
Do you know the muffin man,
Who lives on Drury Lane?
Yes, I know the muffin man,
The muffin man, the muffin man,
Yes, I know the muffin man,
Who lives on Drury Lane?

I know nothing of this Muffin Man character.

I can't interview him like I had planned because he got hit by a bus last year and is six feet underground - the poor bastard. I went on a quest to find someone that could give me any information on him.

I asked Mother Goose for some advice. I knew she could help me out since she has been around the block.

She came through and hooked me up with the names of people to track down. She said to find The Gingerbread Man,

Mary Poppins, Hansel & Gretel, The Big Bad Wolf, The Cowardly Lion, The Energizer Bunny, and The Jolly Green Giant. It took me a few months and a lot of frequent flyer miles, but I found them.

I asked all of them one question: Can you tell me three things about the Muffin Man that people do not know? Strangely, there were no repeat answers.

**

The Gingerbread Man: He still owes me 50 bucks from beating him at rock-paper-scissors. He always smelled like sausage. His cat had two tails.

Mary Poppins: He was a generous lover. He actually despised muffins. He invented the jack-o'-lantern.

Hansel: He made the best doughnuts. He was allergic to pineapple. He cheated at board games.

Gretel: He was so dreamy, like a mix of Ryan Gosling and Batman. His ultimate goal was to beat Super Mario

Bros 2 in one night. He was engaged four times but never married.

The Big Bad Wolf: He was my best friend. He had a huge crush on Betty White. He only lived on Drury Lane for nine months of his life.

The Cowardly Lion: Who? Do you mean the muffler man? That guy is great. He always gives me a great deal. Hold on, I might have a coupon.

The Energizer Bunny: He suspected The Big Bad Wolf of stealing money out of his wallet. We had an annual racquetball game with Cupid. His middle name was Wilbur.

The Jolly Green Giant: He never knew why he was cursed with the name 'The Muffin Man.' His favorite movie was Toy Story. He had a tattoo of an octopus on his lower back.

**

I don't think I know the Muffin Man any better than I did before. That endeavor seems like a big waste of time now. I could have used those frequent flyer miles to go to Aruba. I love Aruba! I went there for my 10th wedding anniversary. I had to drag my wife back home.

Just watch out for those iguanas, they are everywhere! You know…I realized I could have saved a lot of time if I found them on social media.

You live and you learn. Especially when it comes to trusting the Big Bad Wolf. He gave me the tip about Betty White living until 2022. I should have listened to Little Red Riding Hood. She's smart. She skipped 6th grade.

Three Blind Mice

Three blind mice. Three blind mice.

See how they run. See how they run.

They all ran after the farmer's wife,

Who cut off their tails with a carving knife,

Did you ever see such a sight in your life,

As three blind mice?

This nursery rhyme has kept me up at night.

As I am sure it has haunted other people's dreams. The farmer's wife seemed a tad bit cruel.

Was she the type of woman who mutilated animals for fun? Did the farmer know of her troubled ways? Were the mice born blind or was there an accident?

I have a shit-ton of questions but no fuckin' answers. I decided to go right to the source. I tracked down the three blind mice and sat them down for an interview. Their names are Ebenezer, Icabod and Pete.

The Tooth Fairy: Thank you gentlemen for sitting down with me to discuss this question-plagued rhyme.

All three mice: No problem dude.

The Tooth Fairy: I am going to get right to it. Were you born blind or did something happen?

Ebenezer: Do you know you are the first person to ask that question? No one else has had the balls to ask us.

Icabod: Thank you for finally bringing up the elephant in the room.

Pete: There's an elephant in the room? I must be getting old because I do not smell anything.

Ebenezer: No, you idiot. It's a saying. It means bringing up a topic that everyone knows about but won't talk about.

Pete: Oh yeah, I knew that.

Ichabod: To answer your question, we all saw the farmer's wife naked. We were in the middle of a game of tag when we saw her come out of the bathroom after a shower. I have never seen a hump on a woman's back before. The image is burnt into my brain.

Ebenezer: She was one ugly sonofabitch. Talk about your old saggy titties. Hairy moles as far as the eyes could see and weird splotches everywhere.

Pete: I've never seen so much hair down there. It was like she was giving birth to Bob Ross.

The Tooth Fairy: That is disturbing. Now, I can't get that image out of my head.

Ebenezer: It is the last thing we ever saw.

The Tooth Fairy: I am sorry you had to go through that. Now is that when she got the knife and cut off all your tails?

Ichabod: No, no, no. You have it all wrong. Betsy is a sweet and caring woman. The farmer's wife's name is Betsy in case you didn't know. Everybody thinks she is this evil person because of that stupid rhyme.

Pete: She was doing us a favor by chopping off our tails.

The Tooth Fairy: You are going to have to explain that one.

Ebenezer: Since we were blind, we kept snagging our tails in doors, drawers, and everything else that we couldn't see. Our tails were all cut up, frayed, and scarred. She cut them off as an act of kindness.

Pete: I thought they would have grown back by now.

The Tooth Fairy: Mouse tails don't grow back.

44

Pete: Yeah, they do. Betsy said we are like iguanas or sea stars. I was scared to go through with it until she told me that.

Icabod: Pete, she lied to you to make you feel better you big, dumb dope.

Pete: Man, I knew 30 years was too long for it to grow back. I miss my tail. I used it to scratch my ears.

Ebenezer: I used mine in the bedroom with the ladies...if you know what I mean.

Ichabod: What ladies? You haven't gotten laid in 20 years.

Ebenezer: Before we went blind, I was giving out so much tail.

The Tooth Fairy: Nice. Now I must ask this because my wife wants to know. Do you guys know Jacques and Gus?

Ichabod: Of course, they are my 2nd cousins on my mom's side.

The Tooth Fairy: Really? That's so cool. My wife will be thrilled.

Ichabod: No, not really. Why does everyone always assume we know those fools? And in case you are wondering, we are also not related to Mickey, Minnie, Stuart Little, or Chuck E. Cheese.

The Tooth Fairy: Okay, I'm sorry I asked. You don't have to be a dick.

Ichabod: We have gotten that question like 400 times. It would be like if we asked you if you hang out with the Boogie Man.

The Tooth Fairy: I do. He is one of my good friends and he is the godfather to my 2nd kid.

Ichabod: Oh. Shut the hell up.

Ebenezer: Hey, calm down. Don't let this turn into like what happened with Dr. Phil.

Ichabod: Ok. Ok. I'll keep my cool.

The Tooth Fairy: We are about out of time anyway. I must get going. This was great. I appreciate the opportunity to get this rhyme cleared up once and for all.

Pete: No problem dude. Anytime.

Ebenezer: It was a pleasure.

Ichabod: Whatever. I need a drink.

Rub-A-Dub-Dub

Rub-a-dub-dub

Three men in a tub,

And who do you think they be?

The butcher, the baker, the
candlestick maker,

And all of them out to sea.

The men in a tub seems a bit kinky for a nursery rhyme.

I can barely fit in a tub by myself. I am not sure how three grown men squeezed into one.

I circled back to Mother Goose for the truth. She knows the original author's son's father-in-law's best friend's dentist's daughter's niece's swimming instructor.

Since this was the only source I had to go on, I sat this woman down for an in-depth interview. She requested anonymity. I will be referring to her as Sally.

**

The Tooth Fairy: I know that you want to remain anonymous, but you don't look like a Sally.

Sally: I know but it is the most generic name I could think of in the ten minutes before we started. What would you have picked?

The Tooth Fairy: Damn, now you are putting me on the spot. Ummm...... Chloe.

Sally: Holy crap, that is my Stepfather's 2nd cousin's name.

The Tooth Fairy: Shut your pie hole. I hate you right now. I am going to pretend I didn't hear you say that shit. Let's get on with this interview already. How much do you know about this nursery rhyme?

Sally: I know everything. I helped write it!

The Tooth Fairy: I call bullshit.

Sally: You're right. I can't back that up. What I know has been passed down through the grapevine. It could be true, or it could all be poppycock.

The Tooth Fairy: It doesn't matter, people will read anything.

Yeah, I'm talking to you. Yes, you. The one reading this book. Don't act like it's not true.

Anyway…back to Sally.

Sally: What I do know is that the story is always interpreted incorrectly. It is not about three dudes in a bathtub.

The Tooth Fairy: I knew it! My dad owes me fifty bucks.

Sally: In the small town where the story was written they used to have boat races using old bathtubs. Local business owners used to close up shop for a day to compete. I think the winner got some money or a trophy or a key to the city, I don't remember.

The Tooth Fairy: I have always wanted to win a trophy. I suck at most things.

Sally: Sorry to hear that, can I get back to my story?

The Tooth Fairy: Yes, sorry for interrupting.

Sally: There was a contest to come up with a name for the bathtub races. A nine-year-old girl came up with the Rub-a-dub Races.

The Tooth Fairy: This is fascinating. Go on.

Sally: The butcher, the baker, and the candlestick maker were always in the top three to finish the race. I think overall the baker held first place the most.

The Tooth Fairy: With all that context the nursery rhyme finally makes sense. Too bad there wasn't a second verse to explain it all. We will all sleep better at night. Thank you, Sally.

Sally: It was my pleasure. It is not everyday that I get to chat with a half-naked, short, fat man with wings holding a wand. You know it isn't Halloween, right?

The Tooth Fairy: I am the fucking Tooth Fairy!!

Sally: Ohhhh, that makes a lot more sense. I am glad I said something. That would have bothered me for days.

52

The Tooth Fairy: I don't even know what to say. I am going to leave now. I will be in touch.

Sally: Toodles.

Little Jack Horner
&
Jack Be Nimble

Little Jack Horner
Sat in a corner;
Eating a Christmas pie.
He put in his thumb
And pulled out a plumb,
And said 'What a good boy am I.'

Jack be nimble
Jack by quick
Jack jump over
The candlestick

I have to say, this backstory is a little raunchy.

If you have a weak stomach, then maybe you should rethink some of your life choices and grow a pair. Was that too harsh? Ya know what, I don't care. I will do what I want.

Were you aware that the Jack from each of these rhymes is the same person? Of course, you didn't. Not to be confused with Jack from Jack & Jill; Jack & the Beanstalk or Will & Grace. Jack has been an attention whore his whole life. It started at a young age and only got worse in his adolescence. Being an only child did not help especially since his mother believed he was God's greatest gift to Earth. And he was not, he was a douche.

In the first rhyme Jack is not eating a slice of pie, he is eating a whole pie. His mother baked him his own pie every holiday. That is one spoiled brat. That began his phase of fingering things he shouldn't.

Like most young boys he was perverted and curious, two dangerous combinations. Let's just say the cats he had as a kid needed some intense therapy. There was also an incident with a clown at one of his birthday parties but I'm not going into detail about that.

The second rhyme seems innocent enough but don't let that fool you. Jack used to challenge the kids in high school to jump over lit candlesticks. He won 90% of the time. He quickly got bored of this and wanted to do something more extreme. He started to jump over the lit candlesticks at home, buck naked, totally free-ballin' it.

He realized right away that he enjoyed the hot flame grazing his twig and berries. It turned him on, and he got off on it. He did it more and more until his mom caught him one-time mid-jump. His sack got scorched like a marshmallow in a campfire. He never did it again.

Throughout Jack's adulthood, he was involved in many sexual harassment lawsuits. He jumped around from job to job because of this. He was a car salesman, a nightclub DJ, a massage therapist, a Walmart greeter, and many more.

He eventually found his passion in Politics. His sexual urges got the better of him again. He was involved in several scandals. Including one with Judge Judy and three with the cast of Full House. He was forced to take a break from politics. He moved out of the country, living somewhere in South America.

After everything cooled down and the coast was clear he moved back to the states. Just to be safe he decided to change his name. He got back into politics.

He made international news when he ran for Mayor of New York City back in 2013. Yep, Anthony Weiner started life as Jack Be Nimble. With a name like Weiner, how did it go wrong? I feel bad for his mom. I hope she has another son to be proud of.

Little Boy Blue

Little Boy Blue, come blow your horn,

The sheep's in the meadow, the cow's in the corn,

Where is that boy who looks after the sheep?

He's under a haystack, fast asleep.

Will you wake him? Oh no, not I,

For if I do, he'll surely cry.

Have you wondered what the first draft of a children's rhyme looks like?

They must have taken a few cracks at it before they were satisfied with the end result. Most of these rhymes were created in the 1700s.

Naturally, they would change over time through storytelling. A lot of them have Shakespearean roots and don't jive with the way people talk today.

I cashed in a few favors and I was able to dig up the original version of Little Boy Blue.

I am pleased with the version that we all know and love today. The original is a confusing mess. I got it from people that would like to remain anonymous. You can judge for yourself.

**

Insufficient Half-Pint Azure, draw near and waft your trumpet,

The livestock is in the pasture, the bovines are in the grain,

Point me in the direction of that youngster which provides reconnaissance for said livestock.

He is on the nether side of a pile of hay, momentarily comatose.

Will you activate his consciousness? Shucks nay, ncvcr me,

Considering with the condition that I take care of business, he will undoubtedly blubber.

I changed my mind. I think I might like the old version a little better. You never see the word "reconnaissance" used in children's literature. What do you think? Do you like the original or the final draft? Please leave a comment below. Oh, wait, this isn't my blog. Never mind, scratch that idea.

It's Raining, It's Pouring

It's raining, it's pouring,

The old man is snoring,

He got into bed,

And bumped his head,

And couldn't get up in the morning.

I have always found this rhyme to be vague.

I would love to rant about it for at least two pages but that would be selfish, and you deserve better than that from me.

As usual, I did some digging, talked to some folks, and cashed in a few favors to find out the truth behind this old man. The old man and his wife have been dead for quite some time.

However, I was able to get in touch with the maid that used to take care of the household. Dolores is in her 80's now and lives in London, England. Ever since she had a mini-stroke, she has had trouble speaking. We have been communicating via email. Her last correspondence reveals the facts behind this nursery rhyme.

Dear Mr. Tooth Fairy,

It has been years since I worked for Matilda and Jim Parsons (no relation to the actor but I love that show). I hope I remember the facts correctly. The ol' thinker isn't as keen as it used to be. I have been taking Ginkgo Biloba to help with my memory, but I forget to take them. It is a vicious cycle. Oh, how I miss the old days. I was such a fireball. The guys would be on me like a moth to a flame. I could tell you some stories that you wouldn't believe.

The things I could do with my legs. Have you heard of the British pretzel? I invented that move. I once considered a career in the porn industry. I was afraid my parents would find out and never talk to me again. They were deeply involved in the church. I have a theory that I am adopted, and my parents never had sex. I did not mean to put the image of your parents having sex in your head. Darn, I did it again. I do not remember what I am supposed to be talking about. Oh yes, Little Red Riding Hood. That little girl was such a bitch. She must have learned it from her grandma. That wolf did this world a favor.

Speaking of nursery rhymes. Did I ever tell you I worked for Matilda and Jim Parsons? 'The Old Man is Snoring' is about him. They became very kinky in their old age. They had a sex swing bolted to the ceiling right next to the bed! Jim would always bang his head on that thing. What a clutz that man was. Hope to hear back from you soon.

Sincerely,

Dolores Metcalf

P.S. I highly recommend a sex swing. Those things are fun and damn sturdy.

Peter Peter Pumpkin Eater

Peter, Peter pumpkin eater,
Had a wife but couldn't keep her;
He put her in a pumpkin shell
And there he kept her still.

Peter, Peter pumpkin eater,
Had another but didn't love her;
Peter learned to read and spell,
And then he loved her very well.

Even I wanted to know more about this rhyme.

I went straight to the source. I tracked down the infamous Peter and was eager to pummel him with questions. It turns out Peter has extreme agoraphobia and never leaves his house.

I moved on to plan B. I found both of his ex-wives, Brumhilda, the one he put in a pumpkin shell, and Sarah, the one he loved very well.

They had never been in the same room together until this interview.

The Tooth Fairy: Ladies, thank you for agreeing to do this interview. It must be awkward to see each other for the first time.

Brumhilda: You have no idea. All I want to do is slap this bitch.

Sarah: You wanna go? Cuz I will end you.

The Tooth Fairy: I knew this would happen. Knock that shit off right now. Can't you both be civilized adults and let the past be the past?

Brumhilda: I can if she can.

Sarah: I can too but if she even looks at me funny, it's go time.

The Tooth Fairy: Just play nice while you are here. You can do whatever you want to each other after you leave the studio. I could use some fresh content for my Youtube channel anyway. I need to keep my 3 subscribers happy. We all want to know more about Peter.

Brumhilda: He's a sleazy dog turd, what more is there to know?

74

Sarah: He was sweet when he wanted to be. That's why I fell in love with him. What bothered me was his obsession with pumpkin pie. Just about every night he had to have some. And that is not a sexual inuendo. He loved pumpkin pie that much.

Brumhilda: Tell me about it. He tried to make me into a pumpkin pie. Good thing I had my cell phone when he sealed me in that pumpkin shell. 911 thought it was a prank call. I had to call back 3 times until they took me seriously.

The Tooth Fairy: Hey, look at that, you have something in common. Does he do any other weird shit?

Brumhilda: Instead of clipping his toenails, he uses his mouth. You wouldn't think he'd be that flexible but sure enough, he can get that foot right in there.

Sarah: I saw him do that once and it gives me the heebie jeebies every time I think about it. I wish I had a time machine so I could go back and erase that from my memory. What bothered me was he would always emphasize the 'H' in certain words like cool whip, where, why, whore, and whimsical. It drove me nuts.

The Tooth Fairy: Ah, man, I have a buddy that does that too. He thinks he's all smart and shit, but he comes off as an asshole. And that toenail thing is disgusting. So, I can understand why Brumhilda divorced him but why didn't it work out with you Sarah?

Sarah: There was a lot of stuff but mostly because of three things. Peter was a selfish lover. He rarely ever returned the favor if you know what I mean. He started to become a hoarder. He never threw out old newspapers, cereal boxes, or yogurt containers. He also cheated at board games and that was the last straw.

The Tooth Fairy: My wife cheats at board games. I sympathize with you. Now that his agoraphobia has gotten really bad, being a hoarder probably does not help his situation.

Brumhilda: Yeah, the living conditions where he is are atrocious. I had to go over there about a year and a half ago for some closure that my therapist suggested. There is crap everywhere. I couldn't stay there more than five minutes. The smell was getting to me. I told him I would facetime him another day.

Sarah: I bet it smelled like spoiled yogurt and newspaper ink. You couldn't pay me enough money to go over to his place.

The Tooth Fairy: That man has a lot of issues. Do either of you have anything good to say about him?

Brumhilda: He was an amazing kisser.

Sarah: He could hang a picture frame like nobody's business. They were always level.

The Tooth Fairy: At least it wasn't all bad. We need to wrap this up. I have a dentist appointment in twenty minutes. Thanks again for coming in to do this. I have a better understanding of Peter now.

Brumhilda: No problem, this was more fun than I thought it would be.

Sarah: I agree. Want to go get a drink and bury the hatchet?

Brumhilda: Only if we can go to a bar that has a mechanical bull.

Sarah: Deal.

Brumhilda: Wait, did The Tooth Fairy just say that he had a dentist appointment?

Sarah: I was thinking the same thing. Is that like the Easter Bunny going to the vet?

Brumhilda: Ha, you're funny. I think we might become best friends.

Sarah: Awesome, let's go get wasted!

Old Mother Hubbard

Old Mother Hubbard
Went to the cupboard,
To give the poor Dog a bone,
When she came there,
The cupboard was bare,
And so the poor dog had none.

She went to the bakers,
To buy him some bread;
When she came back
The dog was dead!

She went to the undertakers
To buy him a coffin;
When she came back
The dog was laughing.

After years of companionship, the dog kicked the bucket.

Old Mother Hubbard was left to her thoughts and to live out the rest of her days alone. One day she came across a diary that she had never seen before. The diary belonged to the dog.

She was flabbergasted. It is a shame that Old Mother Hubbard died before she could finish reading it.

The diary was placed in storage with the rest of her belongings. I got a hold of the diary through an estate auction.

I also got a bunch of the old lady's nightgowns and necklaces. I like to play dress-up. Don't you dare judge me.

Here are some entries from the diary: I had to rewrite them. The dog wrote the entries in cursive and backwards. It was a bitch to decipher them in the bathroom mirror.

March 21

Dear Diary,

I did it again. I hid the old lady's glasses. She was looking for them for hours. She eventually found them in the fridge! This is becoming my favorite game to play. And she doesn't even suspect that I am doing it. I wonder what else I could do……

April 2

Dear Diary,

She almost caught me trying on her makeup again. I had to pretend like I was eating her lipstick. She hit me with the newspaper and kicked me outside. I feel humiliated, but it feels right putting it on. I guess if I was a female dog it would be okay. Is it wrong to fantasize about being a female dog? I am all sorts of confused.

May 15

Dear Diary,

I taught the cat to play dead too. We freak out the old lady at least once a month. You would think she wouldn't fall for it anymore. At first, she was relieved but lately, she has been getting quite pissed off. Maybe we should stop? Naahhh. I still need to teach the hamster and parrot to play dead.

June 28

Dear Diary,

How come every time I start licking my crotch, she yells at me? I'm stuck inside all the time. It's not like she takes me to the park where I can get some tail. I am so horny all the time. It's not like I have hands. I can only use my tongue.

It is extremely frustrating. What does a dog gotta do to get his hump on around here?

July 9

Dear Diary,

The old lady was watching Lassie again. That dog is smokin' hot. I can't even explain what I would do to that bitch. I can never find it late at night. I think it is only on during the day. I am going to lick myself real good tonight.

August 17

Dear Diary,

I am getting tired of this slop that she keeps feeding me. She gets to eat steak, chicken, bacon, and one time she was eating lobster. I thought the cat might have it better but his food tastes like garbage too. I

wish I could be a famous movie
or television dog like Rin Tin
Tin, Beethoven, or Eddie from
Frasier. I bet they get fed some
good chow.

**

That dog was a dick to Old Mother
Hubbard. I wonder if reading the diary is
what killed her. How did the dog hold the
pen, in his mouth or paw?

Did the cat also have a journal? It is
a shame that the dog didn't include the
year in his journal entries. We don't even
know how many dogs the old lady owned
in her lifetime. Was there ever a Father
Hubbard? Did she have kids? I have loads
of questions that will most likely never get
answered.

Rock A Bye Baby

Rock-a-bye baby

On the treetop.

When the wind blows

The cradle will rock.

When the bough breaks,

The cradle will fall.

And down will come baby,

Cradle and all.

I once again hit up Mother Goose for some information.

I think she is getting tired of me. She pulled out a stack of papers from her credenza and dropped them on my foot.

There were over fifty letters all regarding this one rhyme. And they were all from the same person.

This person was a representative for 'Babies Against Unjust and Unreasonable Treatment.' I found one letter that stood out to me.

By the way, this "person" is a baby.

To whom it may concern,

Our organization represents babies all over the world. We have written several letters prior to this one without a response. We are currently working with some of the best attorneys to remove this nursery rhyme from all literature. Please cease and desist from the use and distribution of this rhyme. It is detrimental to the health and safety of our people.

We are a powerful and influential organization. We do not want to pursue legal action and/or punitive damages. It appears it may just come to that. If you do not believe in our clout or power, feel free to ask Pee-Wee Herman or Steve from Blue's Clues what we're capable of.

Most babies think that nursery rhymes are ridiculous but this one takes the cake. Why would any baby want to be in a tree? How would this help us fall asleep? No one has been able to explain the purpose of this rhyme. It might as well be about holding a baby over shark infested waters. We end up falling asleep to this horrible short story because it is our only way of getting away from it.

As a result, you think we enjoy the rhyme and continue to use it for months creating a vicious cycle. Just because we cannot talk yet does not mean we don't have feelings that matter. I understand the

contradiction that I do not possess the
ability to speak but I can create formal
letters in perfect English.

Babies are extremely resourceful and
do not forget it. Society underestimates
babies way too often. We are capable of great
things. I have so much to say that doesn't
even pertain to Rock-a-bye baby. I need to
focus and stay on point. I don't need to
write down everything that I am thinking. I
hope I edit this before I mail it out.

Most babies grow up with a fear of
heights and falling. This nursery rhyme is
at the top of the reasons why. Roller
coasters are a distant second. Bungee
jumping squeaks in at number three.

A significant number of babies are
deeply affected by Rock-a-bye Baby every
year. These babies grow up to be
lumberjacks. The only mental relief they get
is cutting down the trees that haunted
their dreams. Paul Bunyan is an extreme
example. He has gone through years and
years of therapy. Babe the blue ox is his
emotional support animal.

I hope that I have made myself crystal
clear this time around. If I need to
organize a hunger strike I will. I can have
every baby wake up ten times a night if need
be.
I do not want to abuse my power. Please
be smart. If I do not hear back from you or

your organization within two weeks' time,
well, you don't want to know.

Sincerely,
President & CEO
Tiberius J. Pennypacker

Jack and Jill
and
Humpty Dumpty

Jack and Jill went up the hill
To fetch a pail of water.
Jack fell down and broke his crown,
And Jill came tumbling after.

Humpty Dumpty sat on a wall
Humpty Dumpty had a great fall
All the king's horses and all the king's
men
Couldn't put Humpty together again

The dark underbelly of nursery rhymes shines through here.

Some information may be shocking. Please refrain from reading ahead if you have a weak heart or stomach or are nine months pregnant. If you are nine months pregnant, keep on reading. It might get the kid out.

I did not have to rely on Mother Goose to obtain the details. My Grandmother gave me the full scoop the last time I visited. I trust her even though she pronounces Reece's Pieces incorrectly.

Jack & Jill were fraternal twins. Jack was the hot twin and Jill was a bit dumpy. Jack received all the attention and Jill hated him for it. Maybe she should have lost that freshman fifteen and occasionally threw on some make-up. In High School, he was captain of the football team and voted most popular.

Jill met Humpty Dumpty at one of Jack's football games. He was the mascot for one of their rivals, James Woods High School Fighting Yolks. After that game, Jill and Humpty started dating behind Jack's back. Jill did not tell Jack because she knew he would not approve. Well, yeah, you're hooking up with a giant egg.

He was also the favorite twin. Their mom would never admit it, but Jack got most of the love. Jill was fed up with all the attention that she was not getting. One day Jill snapped and convinced Humpty to 'get rid of her problem.'

Jack falling and breaking his crown was no accident. He was murdered by Humpty Dumpty! I knew Humpty Dumpty was a dick. His facial expressions gave it away. He was so distraught over what he did that he decided to take his own life. A three-foot jump off a stone wall was all that it took.

He left a suicide note. I still do not know how my memaw snagged a copy. This is how it reads:

**

To whoever finds my body,

I am terribly sorry. I am a bad egg. I deserve to be cracked on the sidewalk. I have done an unspeakable thing. Jack did not fall down the hill by accident. I pushed him. I just wanted to break his legs or disfigure him a little bit. I swear I wasn't trying to kill him. Tell my mom that I love her, and I have always hated my name. I leave my Pokemon cards to my brother Lumpy.

With deepest regret,
Humpty Muriel Dumpty

P.S. Please don't let those horses try and put me back together. They have no hands and

will only make a mess. I have
watched them play with jigsaw
puzzles.

**

Humpty did not snitch on Jill. He took full blame. Jill split town as soon as she heard of Humpty's accident. She never got wind of the suicide note. She just assumed the police would pin his death on her somehow.

She bounced around from state to state as an exotic dancer working for local strip clubs. She went by the name 'Tumbles'. No one has seen her in years. Her mom doesn't know if she is alive or dead.

If you have any information on Jill's whereabouts, please call her mom at 555-555-1234. She is worried sick. There is no reward, I already asked.

Aftermath

My childhood memories have been ruined.

This opens a whole new can of worms. My therapist has some work ahead of him. I have always heard that the truth shall set you free. I do not think it applies here. Part of me is glad that I found out the truth.

Another part wishes that I had just stayed home and binged-watched The Golden Girls. Betty White was my celebrity crush. My wife said she would have looked the other way if I got Betty's consent. Her age never bothered me. Her death does, though. I am pretty kinky, but I draw the line at necrophilia.

I am almost positive I have enjoyed a lap dance from Tumbles. I don't quite remember because I am usually drunk at strip clubs.

I want to thank Mother Goose for helping me out and getting me the right information.

It's funny, but I thought she was going to be a little old lady but she's like 6'3" and covered with tattoos. I think the motorcycle and the Hells Angels jacket threw me off.

Let us hope that parents know better than to read these stories to their kids. This book should be hidden away along with the sex toys.

Do you think your parents still use sex toys? Never mind, do not think about that. Damn, now I am thinking about my parents. Oh, the horror!!